12-09

Martin Bridge
The Sky's the Limit!

written by
Jessica Scott Kerrin

Illustrated by
Joseph Kelly

Kids Can Press

To Peter and Elliott, and also to Elliott's story-worthy cousins: Avery, Jackson and Georgia DeAbreu; Stuart, Alexander and Gregory Mackenzie; Jack and Christopher Carlyle; and Christian, Lauren and Aiden Bertuzzi — J.S.K.

Por Lillian y Ernesto, con todo cariño por creer en mi — J.K.

Text © 2008 Jessica Scott Kerrin
Illustrations © 2008 Joseph Kelly

Kids Can Press acknowledges the financial support of the Government of Ontario, through the Ontario Media Development Corporation's Ontario Book Initiative; the Ontario Arts Council; the Canada Council for the Arts; and the Government of Canada, through the BPIDP, for our publishing activity.

Published in Canada by
Kids Can Press Ltd.
29 Birch Avenue
Toronto, ON M4V 1E2

Published in the U.S. by
Kids Can Press Ltd.
2250 Military Road
Tonawanda, NY 14150

www.kidscanpress.com

Edited by Debbie Rogosin
Designed by Julia Naimska
Printed and bound in Canada

Interior art was drawn with graphite and digitally shaded. Cover art was painted with acrylic and pixels.

The text is set in GarthGraphic.

CM 08 0 9 8 7 6 5 4 3 2 1
CM PA 08 0 9 8 7 6 5 4 3 2 1

**Library and Archives Canada
Cataloguing in Publication**

Kerrin, Jessica Scott
    Martin Bridge the sky's the limit! / written by Jessica Scott Kerrin ; illustrated by Joseph Kelly.

ISBN 978-1-55453-158-5 (bound).
ISBN 978-1-55453-159-2 (pbk.)

I. Kelly, Joseph II. Title.

PS8621.E77M358 2008   jC813'.6
C2007-906552-X

Kids Can Press is a Entertainment company

Contents

Earplugs

"I've pulled some strings," Head Badger Bob announced as he read from his overstuffed clipboard. He always saved big news for the end of Junior Badger night.

Martin's stomach did a little leap. He knew that whatever Head Badger Bob had in mind, the sky was the limit!

The Junior Badgers stood in a semicircle, and they all held their breath.

"The Harbormaster has invited our troop to watch this weekend's fireworks from his trawler!" Head Badger Bob boomed.

The troop whooped. Watching from a boat in the harbor meant that they would be right beneath the fiery display!

Dazzling spinners! Whistling missiles! Spectacular sparklers!

Zing! Zang! Zow!

Martin turned to his best friend, Stuart, and gave him a playful punch on the shoulder.

"Ka-boom!" Stuart replied, throwing his arms sky-high. "You'll be plugging your ears for sure!"

Martin didn't mind the tease. Even though he had worn earplugs during last year's fireworks to muffle the thunderous explosions, he had still *ooohed* and *aaahed* along with the rest of the crowd at each brilliant burst of color.

But wait! Martin suddenly remembered that he was expecting company.

"Can my cousin Fletcher come, too?" asked Martin. "He's a Junior Badger from another troop, and he'll be staying with me this weekend."

"One more Badger won't tip the boat!" assured Head Badger Bob. He began to hand out sheets of paper. "These are the instructions on getting to dock," he trumpeted above the hoopla. "See you this weekend!"

"Have I met Fletcher?" asked Stuart as they got their jackets.

"You probably wouldn't remember him," said Martin. "The last time he came, we were all just little. But my mom says we have a lot in common."

A boy flew by with his shirttails flapping and his hair sticking up at the back.

"Hey, Curtis!" Martin called out. "How's Alex?"

Alex was Martin's other best friend, and Curtis was Alex's younger brother.

Alex was at home with the chicken pox.

"He's grouchy," said Curtis as he pushed his glasses up on his nose. "And he's going to give me an atomic wedgie if I forget to remind you guys to come over Friday after school."

"Don't worry," said Stuart. "We'll be there."

"Their fights are getting brutal," Martin said to Stuart after Curtis darted off. "Did I tell you about the purple juice stain?"

"Purple juice stain?" repeated Stuart.

"Listen to this one," said Martin. "I was at Alex's yesterday, and he and Curtis got into a giant shoving match over the last

cookie. Curtis knocked his juice glass onto the carpet right between the two beds! *Spa-loosh!*"

"What did their mom say?" asked

Stuart with a mix of fascination and horror.

"She doesn't know about it yet," said Martin. "But when she does find out ..." His voice trailed off, and Stuart nodded sympathetically.

Everyone knows that purple juice stains are *the worst*.

"What about Fletcher?" said Stuart. "Think he'll be tackling *you* for the last cookie?"

"Not likely!" said Martin with a dismissive wave of his hand. He was certain that Fletcher would be an excellent roommate.

After all, his mom said they had a lot in common.

With that in mind, Martin planned out his week.

On Tuesday, he rearranged the rocket
collection on his bookshelves so that
Fletcher could easily identify the different
space fleets.

On Wednesday, he set up the extra cot
in his room and laid out his galaxy-covered
blanket on Fletcher's bed.

On Thursday, Martin personally selected
a glow-in-the-dark drinking glass for Fletcher

and placed it on the bathroom counter.
Then, as the finishing touch, he fanned out
a handful of the latest *Zip Rideout* comic
books on top of Fletcher's blanket.

Zip Rideout, Space Cadet, was Martin's
favorite cartoon superhero.

By Friday, Martin was all set for his
guest, so he had time to visit Alex. When
he arrived, Stuart was already there.

Martin secretly motioned to Stuart
and pointed to Curtis's carefully placed
pajamas that were covering the purple stain.

"Hi, Martin," said Alex, as Stuart
nodded at Martin's clue.

Alex lay propped up by pillows. He was
covered in pink spots.

"How are you?" asked Martin.

"Lousy," admitted Alex.

"You mean crabby," said Curtis, who was humming to himself as he sprawled on his own bed, leafing through a *Zip Rideout* comic. Curtis did not look up as he said it.

Alex took full advantage by firing a pillow at Curtis's head.

"Hey!" yelped Curtis. "I'm telling!"

"Go ahead, Curtis. Tell," said Alex with deadly aim. "And I'll tell Mom about the carpet."

Martin could almost see sparks fly as Curtis sent a thought dagger to Alex before returning to his comic book.

The boys spent
the rest of the
visit playing Zip
Rideout's supernova
card game, but they
were interrupted
regularly when Alex
yelled at Curtis to
stop humming.

"I'm not
humming!" Curtis repeatedly shouted back,
even though he had been.

At one point, when Alex was out of
pillows to throw, he yanked Mars from the
solar system mobile orbiting above his bed.
He pitched it at Curtis mid-tune. Curtis
ducked, and the red planet rocketed out
the window.

"Hey!" a voice exploded from below.

"Sorry, Dad!" called Curtis. "Alex is throwing planets again."

Martin looked up at the beleaguered solar system. Neptune and Mercury were also missing, presumably lost in earlier intergalactic wars.

Alex whipped back his covers, sending

cards flying in all directions, and stormed to the open window.

"Dad!" he yelled down. "Tell Curtis to get out! We're trying to play a game, and he keeps interrupting!"

Martin knew this wasn't exactly true. But no way was he going to defend Alex's little brother and risk more flying tempers.

Or planets.

"Curtis!" called their dad from below.

"I didn't do anything!" yelled Curtis instantly.

"Come on down, buddy. I need your help in the garden."

"Okay," said Curtis, happily enough. He stuck out his tongue at Alex before scooting from the room.

Martin almost chuckled. Alex and Curtis could sure use a lesson in getting along, he thought smugly.

"Let's finish the game," suggested Stuart, plucking the cards from the floor.

After a few more rounds, Martin laid down the card with the orange planet.

"I win!" he declared. And then, with even more excitement, he added, "We'd better get going, Stuart. Alex's dad said he would drive us home at five o'clock so I can be back in time for my cousin."

The boys gave Alex the official Zip Rideout salute on their way out.

Almost as soon as Martin got home, the doorbell rang.

"I'll get it!!" he shouted, and he bolted down the stairs to the front hall.

His mom had beaten him to it. She was already on the porch, hugging their guests.

"Hi, Fletcher," said Martin in his friendliest voice.

"Hi, Martin," said Fletcher.

He shifted a huge duffle bag from one shoulder to the other, clearly struggling under its weight.

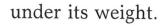

"I'll help you take your stuff upstairs," said Martin. "You're staying in my room."

"Great!" said Fletcher, and he swung the duffle bag toward Martin, almost knocking them *both* over.

Martin heaved the duffle bag onto his shoulder while Fletcher retrieved a second duffle bag from the porch. It appeared to be just as heavy as the first.

Martin wobbled up the steps, one at a time. "What's in here?" he joked. "Books?"

"Yes," was Fletcher's surprising answer.

Martin paused to consider. "But you're only here for two days."

"Right," said Fletcher. "That's why I brought so many. I hope you have sturdy bookshelves."

"Sturdy enough for rockets," mumbled Martin as he struggled through the doorway to his room. "Here we are," he announced.

With relief, he dropped Fletcher's duffle
bag to the floor.

Fletcher took a different approach.
He pitched the *Zip Rideout* comics that
Martin had selected and set his duffle bag
on the cot.

"Do you like Zip Rideout?" asked
Martin eagerly, gathering the comics from
the floor.

"He's okay," said Fletcher flatly. "But I like *real* books better."

Doubt about Martin's roommate began to creep in.

Fletcher whipped open his duffle bag, shoved Martin's rocket collection aside, fleet by fleet, and began to stack his books on the shelves.

Big thick books.

And not one of them had words like "explosion," "slime" or "dinosaur" in the title.

Within minutes, Fletcher had completely rearranged his half of the room.

This bothered Martin, but he was determined not to react like Alex. Instead, he tried a new tack.

"All set for tomorrow's fireworks?" he asked Fletcher. "We'll have a blast being on a boat right beneath them!"

"I suppose. Mom *made* me bring my Junior Badger uniform," said Fletcher grudgingly.

Martin frowned. How could Fletcher not be interested in the fireworks?

Then Fletcher opened the second duffle

bag and began to
invade Martin's
side of the room!

Creeping
doubt gave way
to rising panic.

"That's my
H_2O Faster
Blaster," Martin
blurted when

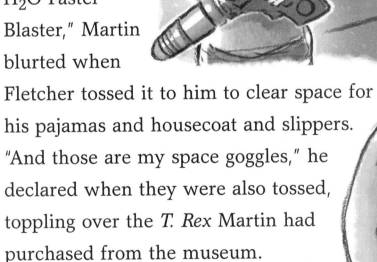

Fletcher tossed it to him to clear space for
his pajamas and housecoat and slippers.
"And those are my space goggles," he
declared when they were also tossed,
toppling over the *T. Rex* Martin had
purchased from the museum.

By now, Fletcher was in the closet,
shoving Martin's clothes to the back to

make room for his own freshly pressed
Junior Badger uniform.

Fletcher paused.

"What's this?" he asked, pulling out
Martin's lobster costume.

"I was in last year's school play,"
explained Martin proudly. His mom had
spent a whole weekend sewing the
elaborate affair.

"You must have looked silly," said Fletcher dismissively.

Martin didn't like Fletcher's tone or the way Fletcher carelessly shut the closet door with a lobster claw jammed in it.

Fletcher didn't notice. He flopped down on the cot, testing for comfort.

Martin was shocked to discover that Fletcher still had his shoes on.

"Dinner, boys!" Martin's mom sang out from the bottom of the stairs.

"You go ahead," said Martin to Fletcher. "I'll be right down."

As soon as Fletcher left, Martin stood his *T. Rex* up again, tucked the lobster claw back inside the closet and quickly brushed the dirt from his blanket.

Dinner was uneventful, except that Fletcher proved to be a picky eater. He had to totally separate the food  on his plate so that his corn did not touch his mashed potatoes. And he refused to try the lemon chicken at all.

Lemon chicken was Martin's favorite.

"So, what are your plans now, boys?" asked Martin's dad playfully after dinner.

Martin quickly ruled out going back to his room.

"Let's go up to my tree fort," Martin offered. "It's filled with stuff I rescued from my mom's last yard sale."

"Is your tree fort high?" asked Fletcher.

"Yes! Really high!" said Martin. It was a bit of an exaggeration, but he wanted to get

Fletcher excited about *something*, since fireworks weren't enough.

"No thanks," said Fletcher flatly. "I don't like heights. I think I'll go read instead."

Read? thought Martin. On a *Friday night?*

Martin spent time alone in his tree fort, testing the reception of his walkie-talkies.

Even bedtime was a disaster. Fletcher somehow used every single towel in the bathroom, and when it was finally Martin's turn to brush his teeth, he was horrified to find that Fletcher had left the cap off the toothpaste, and that the cap had somehow fallen onto the floor.

Behind the toilet!

Cripes!!

"Good night, Fletcher," said Martin in a less-than-friendly voice when he returned to the bedroom.

No answer.

Fletcher was already asleep.

And he was snoring!

Martin had to sleep with a pillow over his head.

The next morning, Martin poured his usual bowl of Zip Rideout Space Flakes. He rubbed his eyes as he dug into the star and comet shapes.

Fletcher strode into the kitchen wearing his matching pajama set.

"Want some?" asked Martin, shoving the cereal box toward Fletcher.

"That stuff will rot the teeth right out of your head," said Fletcher with authority.

He went to the fridge and pulled out a tub of plain yogurt.

He's got to be kidding, thought Martin, his spoon suspended in disbelief.

But no! Fletcher helped himself to a big dollop and added some sliced banana.

Then he sat down and flipped through a book while he ate.

It made for sparkling breakfast conversation.

Martin, who hated both yogurt *and* bananas, had had enough. It was time to ditch Fletcher.

"I think I'll visit Alex today," Martin announced firmly to his mom, who was pouring herself a cup of coffee.

"Good idea. I'm sure Fletcher would like to meet Alex," she replied with a smile that told Martin she still believed he and Fletcher had a lot in common.

Fletcher was so busy reading, he didn't even look up.

Martin sighed.

After breakfast, Fletcher disappeared with his book, while Martin killed time by dropping paper parachutes from his tree fort. His dad drove them to Alex's house later that day.

Martin rang the bell at the front door, but no one answered. He and Fletcher went around to the backyard. Alex's dad was sprinkling grass seed over the patchy lawn where his sons had been learning to stunt jump on their bikes.

"Good thing grass grows quickly," observed Martin.

"But it's going to need lots of water," said Alex's dad. "I was hoping for rain." He looked up at the clear blue sky.

"It's perfect weather for fireworks, though," said Martin, who by now ignored Fletcher's sullenness whenever fireworks were mentioned.

"That's right! The fireworks are tonight," said Alex's dad. He turned to Fletcher. "And who might you be?"

"I'm Fletcher," said Fletcher, shaking hands. "Martin's cousin."

"I can certainly see the family resemblance," said Alex's dad.

What family resemblance? thought Martin. He and Fletcher clearly had *nothing* in common!

"Is Alex upstairs?" asked Martin.

"Yes. Go on in."

As they headed to the back door, Curtis bolted from the house.

"I'm telling!" he shouted as he flew past. But before he *could* tell, a window slid open.

Everyone looked up as Alex stuck out his head.

"Dad! He broke my H_2O Faster Blaster!"

Curtis scuffed at the lawn.

"Curtis, stay away from Alex's things," said their dad in that tired voice parents use when they have to explain something over and over. And then, "Help me finish the seeding. Here are the work gloves you like."

Curtis cheered up immediately. He stuck out his tongue at Alex as soon as their dad wasn't looking.

"Is that your cousin?" Alex called, ignoring Curtis.

"Yes," admitted Martin. "We'll be right up."

When they entered Alex's bedroom, Martin noticed that the purple stain was still cleverly covered.

"How about a round of Zip Rideout's supernova card game?" Alex

suggested brightly, now that Curtis was out of the picture.

Martin nodded eagerly, but Fletcher instantly soured the mood.

"Got anything to read?" he asked. "I don't like cards much."

It was only after Fletcher poked around and found nothing worthy *to* read that he reluctantly agreed to join them.

"One-one-one, two-two-two, three-three-three," counted Martin through clenched teeth as he dealt the cards. He snapped each one down for explosive effect,

42

mostly to blot out Fletcher's grumbling.

Fletcher proved to be a crummy player. He kept laying down the card for Zip's archenemy, Crater Man, which messed up the scoring. And he was clueless when it came to blocking supernovas because he insisted on holding onto all the rocket launch countdown cards!

The game finally ended when Alex played the orange planet.

"I win," he declared, but the thrill was short-lived. Almost immediately, he frowned. "I can't believe I'm going to miss the fireworks."

"You can watch them on TV," said Martin lamely, wishing more than anything that Alex could switch places with Fletcher, who didn't even want to go.

"It won't be the same," said Alex, which was true.

Alex's dad drove the boys home.

"I've asked your parents to take Curtis with you to the fireworks tonight," he explained as he pulled up to Martin's driveway. "We'll be staying home with Alex."

"I'll miss Alex," Martin said sadly, and then, "Thanks for the ride."

Fletcher marched past Martin into the house and headed straight upstairs. Alarmed, Martin followed, and when he entered his room, he gasped.

Once again, his *Zip Rideout* comic books were scattered on the floor. Fletcher lay on his cot reading a thick book with no pictures. And his shoes were still on!

Martin silently calculated how many hours were left until Fletcher went home.

"I'm going to put on my Junior Badger uniform," Martin announced irritably, once he figured out the number. "We'll be

heading to the fireworks as soon as we eat dinner."

"Right," said Fletcher.

But he didn't get up to change until *after* he finished his chapter.

Seething, Martin doubled-checked his math.

The sun was starting to go down as everyone piled into Martin's family van. When they stopped to pick up Curtis, Martin ran to the door and rang the bell.

No answer.

He went around to the backyard and swung the gate open.

"Oh! Hi, Martin!" said Curtis, beaming. He was positioning a sprinkler on the lawn.

In fact, there were a dozen sprinklers scattered around the yard. And Curtis was not in his Junior Badger uniform.

"Aren't you going to the fireworks?" asked Martin.

"No!" said Curtis excitedly. "There's been a change in plans."

"You're just in time for Curtis's big show," said Alex's dad. He was attaching one of the many hoses that snaked across the freshly seeded yard to yet another sprinkler.

The hoses ran to the homes of neighbors all around, and a crowd with keen faces stood by watching.

"Ready?" asked Curtis, practically hopping.

His dad gave him the nod.

Curtis cupped his hands around his mouth. "Alex!" he shouted.

After a short pause, an upper window slid open.

"What?!" Alex demanded.

"Have a look!" shouted Curtis. "I made waterworks just for you!"

Then he and his dad scrambled from house to house, turning on all the faucets.

It was the most marvelous thing!
Sprinklers burst to life, sending arcs of water
gracefully in every direction. *Spisss! Spisss!*
Spisss! The swirling patterns were beautiful,
and so were the hovering rainbows.

The crowd *ooohed* and *aaahed* in delight.

"Holy cow!" said Alex. It was his
favorite expression. "Come and see
this, Martin!"

Martin bolted
through the back door
and up the stairs.

Alex was still
admiring the dazzling
display when Martin
burst in. Alex's
mom was tidying
the room, but she
had stopped to watch the show, too.

"Hi, Martin," she said. "Off to the
fireworks?"

He nodded and squeezed in beside Alex
while she got back to work.

The spraying sprinklers were even
more mesmerizing from above.

"Hey! Who did this?!" Alex's mom
demanded.

The boys turned at her sharp tone. She pointed to the purple evidence, her other hand holding Curtis's pajamas.

Martin braced for impact. He knew that Alex would tell on Curtis, Curtis would be called in and there would be another explosive shouting match.

Alex opened his mouth to answer, but then paused.

He turned back to the window and the waterworks below, where Curtis waved gleefully.

Finally, Alex spoke. "*I* spilled the juice," he said. "It was an accident. Sorry." He returned Curtis's wave.

"Honestly!" exclaimed his mom, throwing her arms up in exasperation. She marched out of the room to get some cleaning supplies.

"You didn't tell on Curtis," said Martin, confused at this astonishing turn of events.

Alex shrugged.

"Look, Alex! Look!" shouted Curtis when he turned on yet another sprinkler, this one spurting zigzags into the velvety pink sky.

"Fantastic!" Alex shouted back. He smiled.

"I don't get it," Martin persisted.

"He's my little brother," said Alex simply.

"A little brother who drives you up the wall," Martin reminded him.

"Not *all* the time," said Alex, looking out the window again. "Have fun tonight," he added.

Martin slowly headed downstairs. He paused at the back door, listening as Alex shouted something to Curtis, who laughed. At that moment, Martin realized how much the two brothers had in common.

If only that were true for me and Fletcher, he thought sadly.

Alex's dad was explaining the situation to Martin's parents as Martin climbed back into the van and slid the door shut. As they

drove away, Martin's mom turned to him from the front seat.

"Here. Before I forget," she said, and

she handed Martin a pair of earplugs.

"What are those?" asked Fletcher.

"Earplugs," muttered Martin. "For the fireworks. I don't like the noise."

"Me, neither!" exclaimed Fletcher.

For once, there was excitement in his voice.

Martin stared at his cousin in recognition. His cousin smiled back.

No wonder Fletcher hadn't been keen about the fireworks! He found the explosions as deafening as Martin did!

And if they both disliked loud bangs, maybe they had a few more things in common.

Good thing the weekend was just getting started!

"Hey, Mom!" Martin called out. "Can we make a quick stop? Fletcher needs a pair of earplugs, too!"

Wormhole

When Martin woke up, his first thought was that his prize should arrive at the post office today! Just to be certain, he bounced out of bed and padded over to the Zip Rideout calendar on his wall.

Zip Rideout, Space Cadet, was Martin's favorite cartoon superhero.

And a bowl of Zip Rideout Space Flakes was Martin's all-time favorite breakfast.

So when the Zip Rideout Trivia Contest was announced, Martin was thrilled. He eagerly ate box after box of the sugary star and comet shapes until he had collected a complete set of cards. Then he mailed them off to the cereal company.

The contest instructions had stated that it would take five to six weeks to receive the out-of-this-world prize: Zip Rideout's Space Race Game, *Deluxe* Edition.

Zip's game boasted a glow-in-the-dark map of the Milky Way, a genuine chip from a meteor, inflatable planets, life-size cutouts of Zip Rideout and his archenemy, Crater Man, and a wormhole, some assembly required.

Martin had charted five weeks on his
calendar and had drawn a rocket on the
square marking
the date that
his prize
should arrive.
Then, as the
days dragged
by, he had
crossed off
thirty-five squares. To Martin's delight,
today featured his rocket blasting off.

This was it!

"Martin!" his dad called from the foot
of the stairs. "Are you on your way down?"

"Onwards and upwards," Martin called
back. It was something Zip Rideout said at
the start of every mission.

He yanked
on his clothes,
then slid down the
railing with flair.

"Your mom has a
surprise for you,"
announced Martin's dad as
Martin entered the kitchen.

Martin's heart started to pound.
His parcel! It *had* arrived! That meant he
would be the first in his neighborhood to
own the game!

"Let's wait and tell Martin tonight," said his mom. "I want to be sure first. Besides, you know he can't keep a secret!"

"What do you mean?" Martin demanded, instantly offended.

"You can't," said his mom matter-of-factly.

"Can too!" Martin insisted.

"Oh, really?" said his mom. "What about my anniversary gift that you spilled the beans about? Or telling the Junior Badgers how Zip's movie ended before hardly any of the troop had a chance to see it? Or informing everyone on the bus about Stuart's fear of clowns?"

Stuart was Martin's best friend.

"Your mom's right, Sport," said his dad, chuckling.

"Okay, okay," muttered Martin.

He poured himself a bowl of Space Flakes and turned the cereal box so that Zip faced him.

Martin's mom took a sip of her coffee.

"I have a lot of meetings today," she said to Martin's dad. "The last one might go quite late."

"No problem," said his dad, layering more jam on his toast. "I'll make dinner tonight. How about a barbecue?"

"That'd be great," said his mom, and she smiled. "You haven't charred something in a long time."

Martin's dad rolled his eyes at Martin.

Bored by this go-nowhere conversation, Martin was anxious to steer back to his surprise, which he was certain was waiting at the post office.

"Do you need to pick up anything on your way home today, Mom?" he prodded.

She stared blankly at Martin for a second or two.

"Oh, that's right! Milk!" exclaimed his mom. She turned back to his dad. "Could you get some? We're almost out."

"Sure," said his dad.

They returned to munching their toast.

Just look at them, thought Martin. They were in cahoots, avoiding *any* talk of his prize. But Martin wasn't fooled. His game *had* arrived! He just knew it!

"Better get a move on, Sport," said

Martin's dad, looking up at the clock. "You're going to be late for the bus."

Martin's cranky-pants driver, Mrs. Phips, hated it when passengers kept her waiting. Martin scooped up the last spoonfuls of cereal, then dashed upstairs to brush his teeth and grab his knapsack.

But when he got to the top of his driveway, the bus already stood rumbling. The accordion door folded open, and Martin reluctantly climbed aboard.

"Shake a leg," Mrs. Phips growled, followed

by her predictable muttering about
punctuality.

Martin hesitated at the top of the steps.
He knew that his mom wanted the surprise

to be a secret. But maybe if he told
Mrs. Phips, she wouldn't be so annoyed
with him.

"I'm getting Zip Rideout's Space Race

Game today," he whispered. *"Deluxe Edition,"* he added for good measure.

"I fail to see how that would make you  late," was her crabby comeback.

Martin swallowed. What a waste of a secret! Ears burning, he made his way to the back of the bus to join Stuart.

"Late again, hey Martin?" said Stuart sympathetically, shoving over to give him room.

"She always makes such a big deal about it," Martin complained as he flopped down.

Then he perked up. No way was he going to let Mrs. Phips's grouchiness take away from his excitement.

"Tomorrow's Saturday," said Martin. "Got any plans?"

"I have to help Mom tidy her props shed," said Stuart, shoulders slouching.

That wouldn't be much fun, thought Martin. Maybe he could help Stuart get out of it. This time, Martin would put his secret to good use.

"Why don't you come to my house instead?" suggested Martin. "I'm getting Zip Rideout's Space Race Game today," he bragged. "*Deluxe* Edition!"

"Are you sure?!" exclaimed Stuart. "You've been waiting for that prize forever!"

"I know!" said Martin. "But Mom's acting all secret-y. Zip's game just has to be it."

"I'll still have to help Mom," said Stuart, "but she'll probably let me off early to come over. After all, it's Zip Rideout's Space Race Game! *Deluxe* Edition! I hear the rules say you can crash land up to five times before you have to surrender to Crater Man!"

"Unless you fly through the wormhole," said Martin with authority. "That means you can do a start-over."

"The wormhole," repeated Stuart in awe. "I can't wait to see it!"

Martin's enjoyment of Stuart's response

was only slightly dampened when he
remembered his mom's words about not
being able to keep a secret.

Oh well, thought Martin. One little
slip-up was no big deal. Well, two. But
telling Mrs. Phips probably didn't count
since she had been such a grump-head
about it. If Martin could, he would fly

through the wormhole for a start-over
and not tell her in the first place.

When the bus arrived at school, they
found Alex, Martin's other best friend,
waiting by the front door. He was sporting
his Zip Rideout space goggles.

"Onwards and upwards!" said Alex.

He gave them the official Zip Rideout salute, which he did every morning. But that wasn't why Martin decided to tell him  about his surprise. In fairness, Martin reasoned, he could not tell one best friend without telling the other.

"I'm getting Zip Rideout's Space Race Game today!" he exclaimed. "*Deluxe* Edition!"

Alex peeled off his goggles. "Really? Today?"

"Yes!" said Martin. "And Stuart's coming over tomorrow to play it. Can you come over, too?"

"Sure thing!" Alex promised. "I just hope I don't end up flying through the exploding yellow nebula. My cousin told me he did that and was stranded on an unknown moon for half the game!"

The bell rang, and the boys bounded through the doors and down the hall to their classroom in hot debate over how to avoid the nebula.

When the principal's voice came over the PA system, everyone hushed.

"Attention, girls and boys. I have a few announcements."

Martin felt great, having told his two best friends about the surprise and seeing them so keen. Imagine if he could get on the microphone and announce his big news to the entire school!

"As you know, we've had a few bicycles stolen from the playground. So, we're getting two new bike racks next week, with enough space for all students who need to lock their bikes."

Dullsville, thought Martin, who bused to school with cranky-pants Mrs. Phips.

"Second, our school janitor wants to 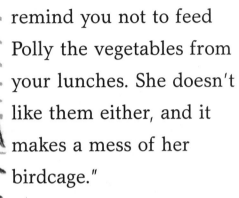 remind you not to feed Polly the vegetables from your lunches. She doesn't like them either, and it makes a mess of her birdcage."

Ho hum, thought Martin, whose mom regularly put crackers into Martin's lunchbox as a proper treat for the school parakeet.

"And finally, I want to remind you that next week some of you will be going to the dinosaur exhibit at the museum with your class. Don't forget that you need to bring in your signed permission slip, or you won't be able to go."

Now *that* was exciting news, but hearing it wasn't the reason Martin felt as if he would burst.

"Have a good weekend, girls and boys."

Then the PA system went dead.

Martin squirmed even more.

"Good morning, class," sang out Mrs. Keenan, their homeroom teacher.

"Good morning, Mrs. Keenan," chimed the class.

The monotony of this daily exchange was excruciating to Martin. His hand practically shot up on its own.

"A question already?" asked Mrs. Keenan, one eyebrow raised.

"Not a question. I have an announcement to make," said Martin proudly.

"Go ahead then," said Mrs. Keenan.

Martin stood for dramatic effect. "Today, I'm getting Zip Rideout's Space Race Game! *Deluxe* Edition!"

A wave of delight swept across the faces in the room.

It was exactly the reaction Martin had hoped for!

"And everyone's invited to my house tomorrow to play!" he added, the last part slipping out in his excitement.

Laila Moffatt, who sat in front of Martin and blocked his view of the blackboard with her big curly hair, twirled around and beamed at him. She did that

about a hundred times a day, which Martin found annoying.

"Sounds great!" she said in her usual pushy way.

Oops, thought Martin. Perhaps he had been overly generous with his invitation. Once again, he wished that he had the wormhole on hand so he could do a start-over.

"You don't like Zip," said Martin flatly.

"But I like games," said Laila in a little voice. She gave him a hurt look before turning around.

Martin sat down. Laila's unwelcome

reply reminded him of how his mom had told him he couldn't keep a secret. He might have been able to defend his decision to tell his two best friends. Now he had gone ahead and told the whole class.

Even Laila Moffatt.

But cripes! Zip Rideout's Space Race Game?! *Deluxe* Edition?!

Who could blame him for spreading the news faster than a meteor blazing across the sky?

Martin tapped Laila on her pointy shoulder.

"You're invited, too," he said, mustering some enthusiasm.

"Really?" said Laila brightly. "I heard you talking about the exploding yellow nebula. I'll be sure not to get stranded!"

It would be just like Laila to win, thought Martin, regretting his invitation once again. He made a note to pull out his book on the night sky when he got home. Brushing up on the universe would give him an edge during tomorrow's game.

"Better turn around," whispered Martin when he noticed that Mrs. Keenan was staring at them.

For the rest of the morning, Martin had a hard time concentrating. He was too busy thinking about game rules involving hurtling meteors and systems of dwarf stars to fully appreciate the importance of adjectives, the steps for dividing numbers, or the names of all five oceans.

Finally, it was noontime. As usual, Martin sat with Alex and Stuart. He began to unlatch his lunchbox, then paused to listen to his friends' conversation. To his dismay, they were chatting about the upcoming soccer game.

How could they have forgotten about his exciting news so quickly?!

Martin silently ate his meal, cookies first, frustrated by their short attention spans. And he barely nodded at Polly, who squawked her thanks for his lunchbox crackers.

When the last class of the day rolled around, Martin was determined to get everyone refocused on tomorrow's big event. Sure, his secret was out, but that only counted if everyone remembered it. His thoughts were interrupted when the art teacher strode into the studio.

"We're going to finish our 'Where I Live' module. So I'd like today's artwork to feature your backyards," announced Mrs. Crammond.

Martin had no trouble deciding what to paint. Art class was his favorite, and Mrs. Crammond had presented him with the very wormhole he sought. Now he could do a start-over and get the class back on track. He quickly set up his easel and had a blast with the paints.

Later, the class walked around admiring one another's work. Martin noticed there were lots of vivid green lawns, flowers on thick sturdy stems and birds that looked like upside-down W's. Pretty standard stuff.

"Oh, my!" exclaimed Mrs. Crammond. "What have we here?" She stood in front of Martin's easel while a crowd gathered around.

Martin's painting was blazing with fiery colors, and it featured people wearing space goggles. Some were climbing up to a tree fort. Others were crouching behind a smoking barbecue or under a picnic table. They all had H_2O Faster Blasters.

"This is the class playing Zip Rideout's Space Race Game at my house," announced Martin. "The first cadet who

successfully outsmarts Crater Man and saves the Orange Planet wins."

"So this must be you," said Mrs. Crammond, pointing to a figure holding a map of the Milky Way. "Nicely done!"

"Onwards and upwards," confirmed Martin, giving her the official Zip Rideout salute.

Other classmates saluted, too, with murmurs of, "See you tomorrow, Martin."

"I'll definitely avoid the nebula," Laila whispered as everyone shuffled off to the next easel.

Then she beamed at Martin. His ears burned.

Martin hastily rejoined the group, but he didn't have much to say about anyone else's work. He was too caught up with Saturday's plans, right up until the end-of-school bell rang.

The ride home was agonizingly slow. Martin's mind raced as the bus rumbled along its route, stopping a zillion times too many. By now he was certain that his mom's story about lots of meetings was a ruse. Instead, Martin was convinced that she planned to pick up his prize from the post office, then get home early and help Martin's dad set up the game in the backyard.

A barbecue!

Good one, Dad, thought Martin smugly.

When he realized that the next stop
was his, he scooped up his belongings. At
the same time, he mentally prepared
himself for what he was about to see.

Maps of galaxies! A meteor chip!
Inflatable planets! Zip Rideout and Crater
Man! The wormhole! Martin's stomach
began to do flip-flops.

He leapt off the bus and saluted to Stuart. Then Martin strode up the driveway, whistling noisily so that his parents would know he was coming. He rounded the side of his house and flung open the gate.

"I'm home!" he announced.

There was no reply.

He took an uncertain step forward.

Still nothing.

A quick survey of the backyard told him everything he needed to know.

No maps of galaxies. No meteor chip.

No inflatable planets. No Zip Rideout and
Crater Man. No wormhole.

Just a smoking barbecue.

Cripes!

A wave of
disappointment hit
Martin. Then he was
hit by another wave,
this one filled
with anger.

"Oh hi, Sport," said his dad as Martin stormed into the kitchen. "Do you want something to drink? I remembered to pick up the milk."

"What happened to the surprise?" demanded Martin indignantly.

"Right. About that," said his dad, suddenly serious. He pulled up a chair and sat down to face Martin. "Your mom didn't  get the promotion she was hoping for."

"The what?" asked Martin, confused.

"The promotion," repeated Martin's dad gravely. "She thought she was going to be offered a job with more responsibility. But someone else was chosen."

"*That* was the surprise?" said Martin, dropping his knapsack to the floor.

"Yes," said his dad, missing Martin's tone. He laid a calm hand on Martin's shoulder. "Your mom's pretty disappointed. We'll have to be extra kind to her this weekend."

Martin frowned. Sure, he felt bad for his mom. He supposed that a promotion with more responsibility was a good thing in the world of grown-ups.

But *he* was the one who had been expecting Zip's game all day long! *Nothing* could be more disappointing than that!

"I'll be up in my room," muttered Martin, who could plainly see that no one would be interested in cheering *him* up tonight.

An even more horrible thought struck Martin as he climbed the stairs. Now he faced the grisly job of calling each and every one of his classmates to cancel tomorrow's plans.

Including Laila Moffatt!

He groaned, desperate for a wormhole to take back the whole day!

Martin lay on his bed, listlessly flipping  through his night sky book and putting off his hateful telephone task as long as possible. He paused when he heard the sound of his mom's arrival.

The low murmur of his parents' voices in the kitchen went on for quite some time. Martin was grateful that his dad was being nice, because Martin was in no mood to put aside his own colossal disappointment.

Then Martin heard his mom coming up the stairs. But something about her footsteps sounded different. They were heavier, perhaps, and slower. She hesitated outside his door before knocking softly.

"Come in," said Martin.

"Got something for you," said his mom.

Martin could tell she tried to say it happily, for his benefit. Only her words

came out all skinny.

She put a parcel down beside him. One quick glance told him it was the game that he had been so desperate for.

"Surprise," said his mom, but there was no exclamation mark. "I came home at lunch and found a notice from the post office saying that a parcel had arrived. I was pretty sure it was your prize, so I picked it up on my way home."

For five long weeks, Martin had dreamed of this moment. He tore into the package at the speed of light.

"Oh, wow!" he exclaimed, pulling out the pieces. "Look at this! And this! And *this!*"

"Very nice," said Martin's mom.

Martin paused.

What was it about her that was throwing him off? Maybe the way she was slouching a bit? Maybe the way she hung her head ever so slightly? She looked smaller somehow.

His mom reached into the box and pulled out — of all things — the exploding yellow nebula. Then she stared into space,

101

as if stranded on an unknown moon.

Something caught in Martin's throat. He had never seen his mom looking so lost.

Perhaps that promotion had meant just as much to her as Zip's game meant to him.

Yet, despite her disappointment, she had still gone to the post office.

For Martin.

And what did I do, thought Martin sheepishly, looking at the game parts tossed higgledy-piggledy about his bed.

"Enjoy," his mom said with a touch of sadness. She turned to go, unaware that she was still holding the dreaded piece that Alex had warned Martin about.

"Wait," said Martin. He took it gently from her. "You'd lose the game if you flew through the exploding yellow nebula."

"Thanks for the tip," she replied quietly.

Martin tossed the nebula back into the game box. His plans for tomorrow were certainly back on track. But having everyone over to play no longer seemed so important.

Martin glanced down and spotted  the wormhole. He realized that what he wanted, more than anything, was a start-over for his mom.

Martin pushed the game box aside.

"How about you and me doing something tomorrow? Just the two of us," he suggested. "The sky's the limit."

"Don't you have plans with Alex and Stuart?" she asked.

Martin knew that if he told his mom the whole class was coming over, she would definitely turn him down.

"No plans," Martin assured her.

Some secrets were definitely worth keeping.

She studied Martin, then gave him her old familiar smile.

"I'd like that," his mom said in a voice more like herself. "Very much," she added sincerely.

"Me too," Martin replied.

Barbecue smoke wafted through Martin's window.

"I better go help your dad," said Martin's mom.

As soon she left, Martin picked up the wormhole and tossed it in with the nebula. Then he dug out the class list from his knapsack, determined to get a jump start on those calls.

Look Up!

To prepare for Zip's Space Race game, Martin studied the night sky. Here are some things you can try to spot. For best viewing, pick a cloudless evening and go to a park or a playing field where city lights won't block your view.

Star or planet?
Stars look like they're twinkling because they're so far away that their tiny points of light are shifted by Earth's atmosphere. Planets don't twinkle because they're much closer and thus appear to be larger,

so Earth's atmosphere has little effect on how they look.

Venus is the easiest planet to spot. It is the brightest object in the sky (except for the moon) and appears low in the west just after sunset. Mars, when it appears, can be easily identified because of its red light.

Comet or meteor?

A comet is made of rock and ice. As it moves toward the sun, the ice thaws, leaving a trail of rock that looks like a slow-moving smudge. Comets are usually difficult to see without a telescope, so if you spot one, consider yourself lucky!

Meteors, also known as shooting stars, are much easier to see. They flash across the sky when Earth passes through dust in space. As dust hits Earth's atmosphere, friction makes the dust heat up and glow briefly before burning out.

Satellite or airplane?

Satellites, made of metal panels that reflect the sun's light, appear as yellowish specks that glide across the sky. Hundreds of satellites orbit Earth taking weather photos, relaying telephone calls, and even spying. Airplanes also glide, but they have flashing lights and appear to move more slowly.

Now that you can identify these simple objects, there's even more to see! The cosmos is brimming with stars that have been mapped out, called constellations. So grab a book about the night sky, look up, and get ready to explore the universe!

Jessica Scott Kerrin, who lives in Halifax, Nova Scotia, has a big secret. She's a terrible speller and also a poor sport when it comes to intergalactic board games. But it's no secret that she loves to watch dazzling harbor fireworks with her husband and son aboard *Cape Fear*, her family's boat. And, unlike Martin, she doesn't have to wear earplugs.

Joseph Kelly wonders why games are so repetitious, need winners and losers or have to end. He and his kids have more fun making up new rules when they play. Try some of their favorites: Cat Scrabble, where the cat chooses the next tile, or Sentence Hangman, where you use whole sentences so the game lasts for days. Then make up your own!

Joseph lives with his family in Sonoma, California. Except for games, he plays by all the rules.

Catch up on all of Martin's adventures!

"Realistic, everyday situations, likable characters and simple stories written in rich language with solid dialogue and humor ... readers will eagerly anticipate every new installment." — **Kirkus Reviews**

HC ISBN: 978-1-55337-688-0
PB ISBN: 978-1-55337-772-6

HC ISBN: 978-1-55337-689-7
PB ISBN: 978-1-55337-773-3

HC ISBN: 978-1-55337-961-4
PB ISBN: 978-1-55337-962-1

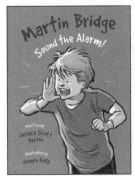

HC ISBN: 978-1-55337-976-8
PB ISBN: 978-1-55337-977-5

HC ISBN: 978-1-55453-148-6
PB ISBN: 978-1-55453-149-3

HC ISBN: 978-1-55453-158-5
PB ISBN: 978-1-55453-159-2

PB $4.95 US / $5.95 CDN • HC $14.95 US / $16.95 CDN
$5.95 US / $6.95 CDN

Written by Jessica Scott Kerrin • Illustrated by Joseph Kelly